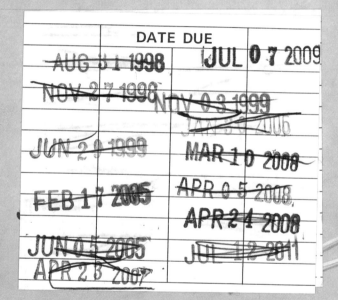

THE
LITTLE MATCH GIRL

Copyright © 1994 by Verlag J. F. Schreiber GmbH, "Esslinger"
Postfach 2 85, 73703 Esslingen (Germany)

Published by Caroline House
Boyds Mills Press, Inc.
A Highlights Company
815 Church Street
Honesdale, Pennsylvania 18431
Printed in Belgium

Publisher Cataloging-in-Publication Data
San José, Christine.
The little match girl / retold by Christine San José ; Hans Christian Andersen ; illustrated by
Anastassija Archipowa.—1st American ed.
[32]p. : col. ill. ;   cm.
Originally published by Verlag J. F. Schreiber GmbH, "Esslinger," Esslingen, Germany, 1994.
Summary : A retelling of the Hans Christian Andersen fairy tale.
ISBN 1-56397-470-3
1. Fairy tales—Denmark—Juvenile literature. [1. Fairy tales—Denmark.
2. Christmas stories.] I. Andersen, H.C. (Hans Christian), 1805-1875.
II. Archipowa, Anastassija, ill. III. Title.
398.2—dc20   [E]   1995   CIP
Library of Congress Catalog Card Number 94-79160

The text of this book is set in 13-point New Baskerville.
The illustrations are done in watercolors.
Distributed by St. Martin's Press

10 9 8 7 6 5 4 3 2

Hans Christian Andersen

THE
LITTLE MATCH GIRL

Retold by Christine San José
Illustrated by Anastassija Archipowa

Boyds Mills Press

The girl had been so cold all day out in the street. Now, through the gathering dark, winds pelted her with snow and bit into her rags. People hurried past her to homes warm with loved ones and fires and Christmas-tree candles and smells of roasting goose. The girl looked up at the golden windows. It was New Year's Eve.

If only she had her shoes. But they had been too big for her. So when she jumped out of the path of a rushing coach, she had jumped right out of them. A boy had snatched them up and raced away.

One last late family came past and—"Oh, please," the girl cried, "won't you buy my matches?"

She held out a bundle towards them. For that was how she earned a few pennies, selling matches. But the family hurried on, as everyone had that day. Unsold matches still stuffed her apron pocket, with not one penny among them.

Without money, she dared not go home. Her father would surely beat her. And, anyway, her house was scarcely warmer than the street. Winds whistled through cracks in the walls and broken windows. She huddled in a corner and sank to her knees.

And then she knew what she could do.

"I'll light a match! Just one. Just one to warm my fingers and glow in the night."

How bright it burned, that match. How it warmed and glowed.

All at once it seemed to the girl that she sat in front of a great iron stove topped with a steaming brass pot. She stretched out her feet to the crackling fire.

But *pfft*, the match went out and the stove went with it.

"Just one more match," the girl promised herself. "Just one more to warm my toes and glow in the night."

This time the wall seemed to melt away, and the girl saw a snowy white tablecloth with gleaming silver and dishes. A magnificent goose stood up from its platter and came toward her.

But *pfft*, the match went out and with it went table and cloth and silver and dishes and goose. And the girl was left staring at the frosty wall.

"Another match!" cried the girl. And now above her spread a Christmas tree that glittered more gloriously than any she had glimpsed through the windows in town. Thousands of candles lit the green branches.

The girl reached towards the tree. *Pfft!* The match went out. But the Christmas lights rose higher and higher...till they shone on the girl like stars. Suddenly, one of them fell from the sky, blazing a streak of fire.

"Someone has died," thought the girl. For her grandmother had told her, "When a star falls from heaven, a soul is climbing up to God." Soon after, her grandmother herself had died, her beloved grandmother, the only one in all the world who had loved her.

"Another match!" cried the girl again. And oh, what joy! Clear, gleaming, gentle, full of love—her grandmother stood before her.

"Oh, Grandmother, take me with you!" begged the girl. "I know that when the flame fades you will fade, too—like the stove, like the goose, like the Christmas tree. Don't leave me here alone!"

Swiftly the girl lit her whole bundle of matches to keep her grandmother near.

The matches burned as bright as day. Grandmother had never been so real and so beautiful. The girl stretched out her hands. She felt wonderfully light. Grandmother folded the girl in her arms and climbed upwards with her, far above the earth.

Above, there was neither cold nor hunger. Higher and higher they climbed, into the light and the warmth. They were with God.

The next morning, a little body was found, icy cold. Spent matches lay around her.

"She tried to warm herself," said someone, "but she froze."

"But see on her sweet-natured face," said another, "a smile of such happiness and love." And they wondered.

No one had seen the beauty that the girl had lit with her matches. No one knew in what splendor she had gone with her grandmother into the New Year.